Magical Islan Adventures

Granny's Big Secret

Katie Pavey

illustrations by Jess Leech

Illustration by Jess Leech (therickettydesk.com).

Title text handwritten by Lucy Massa.

With thanks to literary consultant Claire Wingfield for her invaluable help.

Published by Scolty Books, named for the magical woods where stories blossomed.

katiepaveyauthor.co.uk

Dedicated to my mum, Sandie; my dad, Colin; my sister, Kirsty; and my husband, Matt. All without whom this magical adventure would not have been possible.

And of course to my wonderful pupils at Duddingston, without whom the book might still not have a name! Thank you P5a.

How to say:

Aine – Awn-yah

Aerwyna – Er-wih-na

Creag – Kriy-ag

Draoid – Dra-oi-d

The ferry pulled in to Brodick harbour and Aine scanned the crowd for Granny Sundie. She saw Murdo first, in his tartan jacket, tail wagging furiously. Then she saw Granny, her wild black-and-white streaked hair piled high on her head, wrapped with a violet ribbon to match her eyes. She was wearing tartan trousers that matched Murdo's jacket. Aine called the old dog's name. His ears twitched when he caught the sound of her voice and

barked his response.

Granny lived in an older fisherman's cottage in Corrie that she had painted purple last summer. Aine loved it, even the special way Granny had to open the front door, with a sigh, a kick and a shove. She particularly loved her granny's garden. You had to cross the road to get to it but it was long and flowed into the sea at the other end, perfect for playing fetch with Murdo. Aine could spend hours

throwing the ball for him. It was the first place she headed, with Murdo hot on her heels.

Throwing the disintegrating tennis ball, she caught something out the corner of her eye, grey and shiny in the water. Seals! Lots of seals! All looking at her. Aine waved at them and some seals responded with a flap of their flippers.

What Aine didn't see was the rock-like creature, watching her from the forest behind Granny's house.

Next day was a warm one in Arran and was perfect for Aine's first day of her summer holidays. She had been coming here for nine years, but this was the first time by herself without her parents. She loved walking in the woods, hunting sea anemones in rock pools and pony trekking through the hills and woodland that circled Arran.

That morning, Aine decided she wanted to go looking for fairy houses (also known as toadstools) and Murdo had no objections. He loved walking with Aine. She was always quicker than Granny Sundie, and she found the best twigs to throw. As they got deeper into the woods, the temperature dropped.

"Aine," the wind whispered through the trees. Aine stopped. So did Murdo. She was sure she'd heard someone call her name. The silence was broken by Murdo growling . . . at a rock!

As Aine tried to grab Murdo's collar, the rock moved and shifted. Suddenly a goblin with rock-like skin, grey eyes and moss growing out of his back stood in front of her.

"You are Aine?" he coughed.

She nodded her head, not quite sure if this was real.

"Do you know where Aerwyna is? We were told you did."

Aine looked around her and saw that what she had thought were rocks were now surrounding her. "The only person I know is my granny, and she's called Sundie. I could ask her?"

Just as the goblin was about to answer, they heard a twig snap as someone walked towards them. It was Granny Sundie.

Aine ran towards her granny with Murdo hot on her heels. Granny met Aine with a hug and pushed

Aine's mane of wild, liquorice black hair out of her face.

"I thought I'd join you, sweet pea." Granny Sundie took Aine's hand, glancing behind her, sending a silent warning to the goblins not to follow them with a look like fire. Their walk pulled them deeper into the dense forest as their hunt for fairy houses continued.

As they walked, Granny pointed to the peach fuzzy ferns that captured the dew and to the playful, squawking magpies. Then she pulled aside a branch to show Aine the tiny stack of sticks she promised covered the entrance to the hidden fairy kingdom, but Aine was only focused on the rocks that were soundlessly rolling behind them.

After lunch, Aine was drawing the goblins in her bedroom. She saw movement outside and wondered if they were back. Instead, she saw Granny in the garden. Granny was in her gardener outfit of dungarees, checked shirt and green wellies. She seemed to be burying something. Soon, Aine noticed that there was an army of seals popping up around the rocks at the bottom of the garden. Granny approached but the seals' fat bottoms stayed glued to the lawn, and as Granny spoke they nodded their whiskery faces and their watery eyes told Aine they were listening intently to Granny's words.

Just then a boat went speeding past, frightening the seals, causing them to find protection under the water. Granny was surrounded by a bright, white light when, as if by magic, the sky got dark as a storm started rolling in. Aine knocked on the window to warn her granny as colossal raindrops plopped to the ground. She ran down the stairs and picked up the big golf umbrella from next to the front door. By the time she managed to wrench the door open, Granny was crossing the road. What Aine would have seen if she had stayed looking out the window was a purple light surrounding her granny and her violet eyes shining luminously as she encouraged the storm to chase the boat that had frightened away her friends.

The next day, Aine was making a mess in her granny's kitchen, trying to bake cookies for the goblins – who Aine had decided should be her friends. She was washing her hands in the sink when she looked up and found herself face to face with a giant, white stag. Its antlers, fuzzy like a peach, stretched into the sky. It snorted at her before heading back towards the forest. Aine made her way to the door and stepped outside.

The stag, approaching the forest line, turned to look back at her, beckoning her to follow it with a nod of its head. Aine followed the stag into the woods, but it always stayed just out of reach, pulling her deeper and deeper inside. Eventually it stopped, in the middle of a wild-flower meadow. The clearing was surrounded by Rowan trees and Whitebeams.

The sun shining on the meadow highlighted the yellow iris, the purple loosestrife and the creamy-white flowers of the meadow sweet. The birds were serenading Aine with their sweet song when the quiet was disturbed by the sound of rumbling. Aine had no time to enjoy the quiet; rock goblins came racing in and surrounded her like a cold, grey river.

"Hello again, Aine, granddaughter of Aerwyna."

Confused, Aine turned to face the rock goblin who had spoken. He was taller than the rest and definitely looked 'rockier', than the others. He had what looked like a large hat made of twigs and feathers and there was definitely a bird living in it! A flash of bright light made Aine blink. The meadow was filled with movement. Fairies!

The one nearest to Aine had hair like fire, what looked like scales on her clothes and eyes like a dragon, which were also the colour of loosestrife flowers. There was another fairy whose silver hair floated out behind her, her eyes the colour of sapphire and shining fiercely. Still another, who had flown to be at Aine's shoulder, had deep, red hair, the colour of copper. His limbs long and lithe like branches of a Rowan, his emerald eyes fixed

carefully on the rock goblin. They moved aside to let the dragon fairy through.

"I am Draoid, leader of the fae. You are on our land and I order you to leave. This girl is under our protection!" Her voice roared like fire.

"I am Creag, leader of the goblins and I need Aerwyna. If I can't get her, her granddaughter will do."

"She knows nothing that will help you. This little girl doesn't even know who Aerwyna is!" the fairy retorted.

"But we saw Aerwyna bring in the storm and then this little girl ran out to help protect her from the rain, she must be fae too."

Before Aine could ask what he meant and without warning, a goblin grabbed Aine and started to run, but Draoid was quicker. She stopped the goblin, surrounding it with fire.

As the two sides prepared to battle, the sky darkened again, thunder rumbling in the distance. Granny Sundie walked into the clearing, her eyes shining a bright violet.

"Enough," her voice thundered. Both sides fell still. "My name is Aerwyna, Queen of fairies, friend of the sea. Draoid, I appreciate your help but I know what these goblins want. My friends, the selkies, told me. I can help."

Creag made his way towards the Queen. "Thank you ma'am. We have lost so much of our home already to the hoo-mins. We appreciate any help the fae can give us." The sky lightened, the thunder stopped and the birds started their singing once more.

Aerwyna smiled lovingly at him. "Yes Creag, I fear this is something which will harm us all if we don't act quickly, but first I must speak with my granddaughter."

Granny Sundie took Aine's hand. Murdo had followed Granny into the woods and now settled at their feet. "I think I have a little explaining to do! This will be hard to understand, and you must promise not to tell anyone, not even Mum and Dad – they don't know yet. You see, your granny is really a 3000-year-old fairy, Queen of the Fairies to be exact. 70-odd years ago, I left our home as I had fallen in love with a human." Aine wrinkled her nose and Granny Sundie chuckled softly. "I always meant to come back but then we had your dad, and then his brothers and eventually I felt more at home in the human world than with the fae. Recently my selkie friends have been visiting me, telling me about the impact humans are having and how we must stop it."

Aine nodded. "We learned lots about that in

school, Granny. What can we do to help? And what are selkies? Are they the seals? I saw you talking to them."

Granny smiled. "Och my wee curious girl, yes the selkies can look like seals but can also take the form of humans. With that kind heart and curious mind there must be some fae in you!"

"Do you really think so?"

"Aye I do. And I have some ideas for what we can do to help but for now I can hear the fae, and they are very excited that we are both here. They want to throw us a party. Would you like that?" Aine looked around and noticed that the fae and goblins were chatting excitedly and looking their way.

Nodding her mass of black curls, Aine's toothy grin told granny all she needed to know. With a flick of her wrist, a nod of her head and a wrinkle of her nose, the meadow began to transform around them.

So as day turned to night, the fae had a party. Lights twinkling magically, as if the stars had fallen, fae dancing with goblins, goblins dancing with fae and there was even a surprise visit from the Selkies, all under the watchful eye of the beautiful, white stag.

Granny Sundie or Queen Aerwyna was standing chatting to him and other mythical creatures, dancing with fairies and arm-wrestling goblins, her purple aura shining brightly.

Aine spent time with Draoid, getting to know the dragon fairy (who was secretly her favourite!) As Draoid lit the meadow with a click of her finger, Aine stroked the cotton soft fur of the white stag, and marvelled as the table filled with her favourite foods.

Then she enjoyed the seemingly endless treats – everything she loved like chocolate, fairycakes, sweets and the most delicious, delicate sandwiches.

By the first light of dawn, Aine had fallen into a deep sleep, resting against Murdo, whilst the pup had forty winks, resting his head on his paws. Granny Sundie made her promise to the Rock Goblins to help however she could. Then whispered a quiet spell, which gently lifted Aine and Murdo into the air, floating them back home.

When Aine woke in her own bed, she wondered if she had dreamt everything. She walked down the stairs, yawning. She was just about to tell her granny about her bizarre dream when she noticed that the dishes were washing themselves. She stared at her granny, open-mouthed. "It was all true? You are the Queen of the Fae?"

"Yes, sweet pea."

A smile spread across Aine's face. "This is going to be the best summer ever!"

Granny laughed and Murdo barked in agreement.

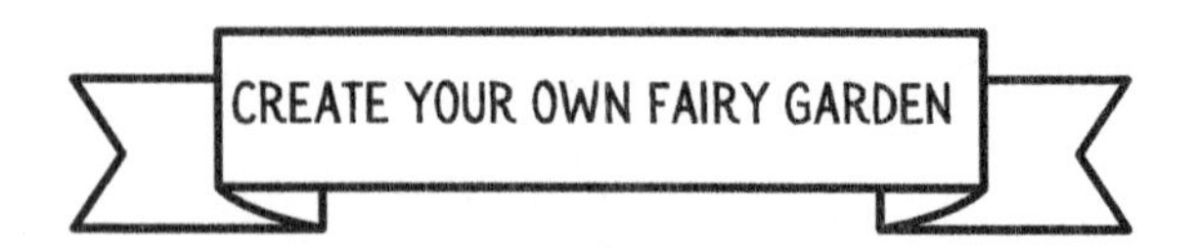

You'll need a die, a piece of paper, a pencil and colouring-in pens.

Instructions

Roll the die and whichever number it lands on, add it to your picture until it's complete.

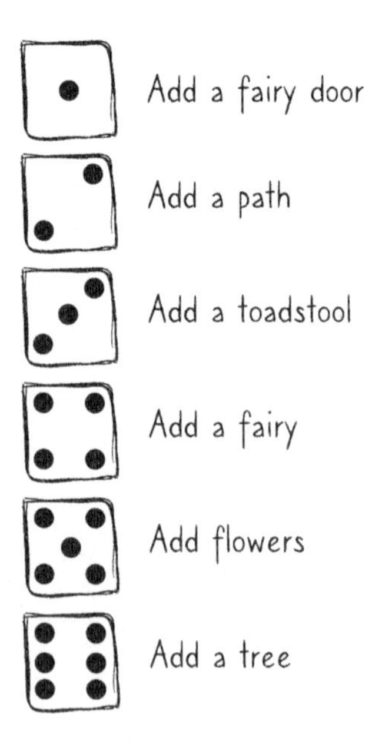

Hold your own fairy tea party

Want to have your own tea party like Aine? Here is a list of some of the food they had. I wonder if any fairies will come and join you? Or maybe Creag and his rock-goblin friends.

- Flower-pot cupcakes
- Fairy twigs (also known as pretzels)
- Chipmunk chips (or banana slices)
- Toadstools (strawberries with cream cheese spots and a marshmallow stalk)
- Fairy wands (wooden skewers, grapes, blueberries, strawberries and watermelon cut with a star-shaped cookie cutter)
- Fairy bread (white bread, butter and hundreds and thousands)
- Pixie-dust popcorn (sprinkles, white chocolate chips, bag of popcorn)
- Rainbow fairy white chocolate bark
- Cucumber sandwiches (Murdo's favourite!)

Or just anything else you fancy. Fairies and rock goblins will eat anything!

Dearest Reader,

Thank you for coming on Aine's magical journey. I hope that you enjoyed it as much as Aine enjoyed her fairy tea party. Granny and Aine will be back soon on another adventure around the Scottish Islands. Please consider spreading the word and leaving a review of this book on Amazon or Waterstones online.

You can also check out Aerwyna's story at www.katiepaveyauthor.co.uk. You might spot some familiar faces there, too.

If you'd like to share your fairy garden pictures, any actitivties inspired by this book or just say hi! you can tag me in @katiepaveyauth1 on Twitter or @katie_pavey_author on Instagram (ask your grown-up for permission!)

See you next time!

Katie x

Printed in Great Britain
by Amazon